DOG DIARIES

BUDDY

D0396031

DOG DIARIES

DOG DIARIES

BUDDY

BY KATE KLIMO • ILLUSTRATED BY TIM JESSELL

RANDOM HOUSE 🏠 NEW YORK

The author and editor would like to thank Craig Garretson,
manager of communications, and Bruce Johnson, volunteer archivist,
The Seeing Eye, Inc., for their assistance in the preparation of this book.

Text copyright © 2013 by Kate Klimo
Cover art and interior illustrations copyright © 2013 by Tim Jessell

Photographs courtesy of: The Seeing Eye, Inc., pp. 138, 139, 140; Tennessee State Library
and Archives, pp. 137, 141

Visit us on the Web! randomhouse.com/kids

Educators and librarians, for a variety of teaching tools, visit us at
RHTeachersLibrarians.com

Library of Congress Cataloging-in-Publication Data
Klimo, Kate.
Buddy / by Kate Klimo ; illustrated by Tim Jessell. — 1st ed.
p. cm. — (Dog diaries)
Summary: A German shepherd describes her life as the first guide dog trained
to serve the blind.
ISBN 978-0-307-97904-9 (pbk.) — ISBN 978-0-307-97905-6 (lib. bdg.) —
ISBN 978-0-307-97906-3 (ebook)
1. Guide dogs—Juvenile fiction. [1. Guide dogs—Fiction.
2. German shepherd dog—Fiction. 3. Dogs—Fiction.
4. Human-animal relationships—Fiction.]
I. Jessell, Tim, ill. II. Title.
PZ10.3.I62Bud 2013 [Fic]—dc23 2012011088

Printed in the United States of America

20 19 18 17 16 15 14 13 12

First Edition

For Fred, a German shepherd . . .

in his own mind

—K.K.

For Molly, sweet on books and dogs

—T.J.

Contents

1

Kiss

I have always known one thing for certain and that is this: I am no ordinary dog.

I am a German shepherd, and German shepherds are a breed apart. We are noble. That's what the Lady Boss, Mrs. Eustis, always said. From the time we were puppies, she would tell us—and anyone else who would listen—that it was a Criminal Waste for dogs as strong of character and as intelligent and energetic as German shepherds to lie on a rug before a fireplace chewing a rubber ball. German shepherds were smart and talented enough to do Important Work. And we, Mrs. Dorothy Eustis's German shepherds in particular, were destined for Great Things.

I started out in life with the name Kiss. I was born in a kennel in Switzerland, where the air had a crisp bite to it, in a place called Fortunate Fields. There were over a dozen of us dogs in the kennel at any one time. Dorothy would rear us and train us and then send us out to work for police forces and armies and post offices and such. Dorothy's dogs were famous all over Europe. I wasn't famous then. I was just a pup. But I was a smart pup, if I do say so myself. I wasn't many months old before the trainers could say, "Here, Kiss," and I went to them. When they said, "Sit, Kiss," I sat for them. When they said, "Down, Kiss," I lay down for them with my nose resting on my paws. These were easy games. What else did they want to play?

The Lady Boss always had a steady stream of guests at Fortunate Fields, friends and family and people who were just plain curious about the work she was doing with dogs. Dropping in on the kennels was the highlight of their visit. The Lady Boss was very proud of us—and with good reason.

"It's important for the young dogs to get used to all kinds of people," Mrs. Eustis would explain to her guests. So we all got a chance to meet a regular parade of individuals: women wearing strong perfume and sparkly jewelry, tall men wearing black hats, short men with long mustaches, children with grabby hands, and people with loud, booming voices. *You can't scare me* has always been my motto.

"We must constantly challenge these dogs," the

Lady Boss would say to her guests. "The more tests they pass, the more qualified they become to do Great Things."

I wanted to do Great Things so I did my best to pass every test. Tests were the best game of all.

"Here, Kiss-Kiss!" the strange people would say to me, holding out their hands. Dogs who jumped up on people and licked them were discouraged with a sharp word from the Lady Boss or her trainers. I didn't care to be spoken to in that tone. So I would walk up to the strange people, sniff their hands, wag my tail, and then politely sit. The object of the game was clear: don't jump all over the people.

The Lady Boss also brought in cats. Wagonloads of cats. Some of the dogs would growl and pick fights with them. But I never did. I let those cats be. I didn't trust them. Those cats were just there to test us. I left squirrels and birds alone, too, much as I would have liked to chase them. I was pretty sure that Not Chasing After Things was the object of that game.

Once, the Lady Boss brought in a man with a stick. We learned later what the stick was. It was a gun. Have you ever heard a gun go off? It makes a loud *boom* and a very bright spark. We dogs have oh-so-sensitive ears and eyes. When the gun went off, some dogs howled and bayed and hid behind their paws. I sat on my haunches and stared at the gun without even blinking. I wasn't going to let a gun beat me. I could play the Sit Still with the Gun game as well as the next dog—and maybe even better.

One night, though, it was another story. On this occasion, a thunderstorm almost won. If you have ever experienced a mountain thunderstorm, you will understand why. Rain gushed from on high and flooded the dog runs. Thunder rumbled down the steep mountainsides. Pitchforks of lightning jabbed at the earth. In the kennels, we shepherds huddled in a heap in our little shelters and waited for it to go away.

Then some trainers in rain gear came to the kennels. They attached leashes to our collars and took us all outside to play Walk in the Storm! Some of the dogs yelped at the lightning and howled at the thunder and tugged and pulled at their leashes, trying to get back into the kennels. But as soon as I was outside the kennel fence, I calmed right down. I turned my muzzle up, opened my mouth, and let the rain guzzle down my throat. I knew the trainers would never have us play this game if they thought any harm could come to us. We were valuable animals! And, sure enough, all I got was soaking wet.

And lots of praise for being so brave. The trainers used up a lot of towels that night drying us off.

In the days and months that followed, some of the young dogs my age left the kennel and didn't come back. I asked where they had gone.

Bruno left because he yelped at the lightning, my friend Gala said. When it came to guessing what the humans were up to, Gala was one smart German shepherd!

Oh, I get it now! I said. I was a pretty smart shepherd myself. *Heidi left because she bit that little boy and growled at the man in the white collar and black coat.*

Exactly! said Gala. *And Sophie left because the gunfire made her whimper. They are not destined for Great Things, like us. They are going to become . . . Pets. That is not our fate.*

No, I said. *I wanted to whimper when the gun*

went off, but I knew it was a game, so I didn't.

Me too! said Gala. *We're still here because we're smart.*

And brave. We're German shepherds! I said, puffing out my tawny chest.

That was why I was so surprised when, one day when I was a little over five months old, a farmer came into the kennels and pointed his finger at me.

"Is this the clever girl who's going to help me with my sheep?" he asked the Lady Boss.

"Yes," the Lady Boss told him. "I think you'll find our Kiss a very helpful shepherd."

And then, before I could lift a paw to scratch my ear, I was leaving the kennels, saying goodbye to Fortunate Fields, to the Lady Boss, to the trainers, and to all my noble canine companions. I was riding off in a rickety horse-drawn wagon with a farmer! I turned my head and looked back at the kennels. There was Gala, staring out sadly through the fence.

Farewell, my friend, I said. *See you again soon . . . I hope.*

Don't worry, Kiss, Gala said. *Lots of us are sent to work on farms. It's good for us. It makes us strong and healthy and even more obedient. You'll be back.*

On the other side of the mountain, as I soon discovered, a new life awaited me, and a new game. This game was Help the Farmer with the Sheep. It sounds easy but it wasn't. Those sheep were silly—and stubborn! They dillied. They dallied. They stalled and meandered. It seemed as if each one wanted to move in a different direction. The object of the game, as the farmer explained it to me in those first few days, was to run around and keep those sheep in a tight knot, all moving in the same direction toward a pasture or pen. It was

hard, challenging work, but I had to stay calm. If I got excited, the sheep would lose their heads and disappear quicker than kibble in a kennel bowl. The sheep were terribly naughty. As much as they sometimes deserved it, I couldn't bite them or scare them to make them obey. "Easy does it," like the

farmer said. I had to keep a sharp eye on them and make sure none of them wandered off or got lost. When they wandered, I would race ahead of them and herd them back to the flock. A lost sheep is a sad thing. Oh, how it bleats and cries! And it's a sad thing for the farmer, too. Those sheep are valuable.

"My sheep are the most valuable things I own, Kiss," the farmer explained. "You need to help me hang on to them."

Naturally, I took the game very seriously. That's what a well-trained German shepherd does. It was a tiring game, too. I was on my feet from dawn to dusk. Occasionally, I would lie down in the grass to rest. But before I knew it, those sheep would start to scatter and I was up and at it again, pulling them back together. What would they have done without me?

When I work hard, I need to rest hard. I'll never forget the end of my first day on the farm. I was so tired I couldn't move. I was lying on my side in the barnyard when the farmer's wife came to the front door of the farmhouse.

"Aren't you hungry, Kiss?" she asked, and she banged a pan with a wooden spoon.

I lifted my head. *Who, me?*

"Yes, you, girl!" the farmer's wife said.

I heaved myself to my feet.

"Thatta girl!" She opened the door, and delicious smells floated out to me from inside the house. Was she inviting me inside?

"Come on, Kiss!" she said. "Time to eat."

Well, why didn't you say so in the first place? I'm never too tired to tuck into some tasty food. I trotted into the farmhouse. In the kitchen, the farmer's wife fed me scraps from the table. People Food! We were almost never fed People Food at Fortunate Fields. The Lady Boss had some very definite ideas about canine nutrition, and none of them involved pork rinds and gristle. If you ask me, People Food is the perfect food.

After dinner, I stretched out at the farmer's feet on the rug before the fire. The farmer smoked his pipe and told me I was a good dog. That's always nice to hear. But I couldn't help but notice that there I was, lying on a rug before a fire. All I was missing was a rubber ball! Was this a Criminal Waste of the character and intelligence of a German shepherd? Maybe so. But I wasn't a quitter. I would give the farmer and his new game my all.

I helped him through the summer, fall, and winter of that year, right into the spring, when there was a new game to play. I helped round up the woolly sheep and herd them, one by one, to the barn. There, they got their lovely wool shaved off. Poor sheep! Seeing them get the shears put to their tender pink flesh like that? I was glad I was a shepherd and not a sheep!

After we played the Shearing Game, the farmer rested his big hand on my head. "Kiss," he said, "I'm going to miss you, girl. But it's back to

Fortunate Fields you go, first thing tomorrow."

My ears perked up. No offense to the farmer or his silly sheep, but my heart soared when I heard the news.

2

THE GUIDING GAME

It was a different Kiss returning to Fortunate Fields that spring. To begin with, I had reached my full growth while putting in my time at the farm. My chest was broad and deep. My coat was long and shiny. And the many months of herding sheep had made me strong. I was serious, too. I wasn't a playful puppy anymore. I was a full-grown German shepherd used to following directions.

While I couldn't quite put my paw on it, Fortunate Fields had changed, too, during the time I was gone. The air rang with excitement. Gala—bless her shepherd heart—did her best to fill me in.

Wait till you see Jack! she said. *You probably don't remember him. He's the head trainer. The Lady Boss sent him away when we were just puppies. He went to Germany, the land of our forefathers. In Germany, they are training us shepherds to play all sorts of important games, like Carry the Message and Track Down the Lost Child.*

Those sounded like good games to me. I wanted to play them, too.

Gala went on. *Jack is back to train us to play these games. They are important games, but only the brightest and bravest of us will play the most important game of all. And that game, according to the Lady Boss, is Guide the Blind.*

Then that's the game for me, I said to Gala.

Me too! she said.

Because we're the brightest and bravest! I said.

Because we're German shepherds! Gala said.

I liked Jack right off. I could tell he understood dogs. You might say that he had been studying us for so long, he smelled like a dog and sometimes acted like one, too. And, if you ask me, with those loose, hanging jowls and big, floppy ears of his, he even *looked* like a dog. He sniffed around me, trying to figure out how many games I knew and how many he would have to teach me. When he told me "Sit," I sat. When he said "Down," I lay down. I came when he called. When he looked me in the eye, I gave him my absolute attention no matter what distractions came up, whether it was the maid shaking out a mop or a hawk diving for a field mouse.

"You're a good, steady girl, aren't you?" Jack said, ruffling the fur on my neck.

You bet I am. Smart, too. Want to teach me some new games? I said, wagging my tail eagerly but not *too* eagerly. No one liked a dog who was too eager.

Then Jack strapped a newfangled harness on

me. I had seen other dogs wearing these things at Fortunate Fields. They grumbled about them in the kennels. Now that I wore one, I could understand why. It was stiffer and heavier than our usual training harness. Attached to a metal loop on the back—in place of a light, loose leash—was a big, heavy handle for a human to hold. It felt awkward at first, but it also felt like a serious piece of business.

Sure enough, the next thing Jack did was put his hand on the harness and say, "Kiss, old girl, this is your Working Harness. When you have it on, you're on duty. Let's see what you can do. Forward," he ordered.

No one had ever given me this command before, so I sat and waited to get a better idea of what he wanted. Jack pushed the handle and gave me a nudge.

Got it. I stood up and walked. I took a few steps and then headed off toward a nice, fragrant spruce tree I had always been rather fond of.

"Wrong. Do not veer off to the side. Go directly ahead in a straight line," Jack said in a stern voice. He popped the leash. That pop—a sudden, quick tug—didn't hurt, but I will say this: it did get my attention. I knew that whatever he was trying to tell me, I had to listen harder and try to understand.

"Forward," Jack said again. This time, I tried going toward the garage and I got myself *another* pop for my trouble.

"Forward," Jack said a third time. That Jack was single-minded.

I heaved a sigh. *Okay,* I thought. *If not toward the tree and not toward the garage, then where?* This time, I went *between* the tree and the garage. And *this* time, I didn't get the pop. This time, I got an enthusiastic "Good girl, Kiss!"

My, my, did I love the sound of that!

We walked together. Or rather, I led and Jack followed slightly behind me. I felt the weight of his body as he stood very straight and leaned back holding the harness handle. I had to pull him to get him to move forward. It had taken me a while—and more than a few pops—to understand that *Forward* meant walk ahead in a straight line. After that, by the same slow process, I learned to turn right and left on command. The other thing I learned was to Haul Up and Stop whenever we came to a curb. This guiding game was a cinch once I got the hang of it.

"The reason we train the dog to haul up and stop," Jack explained to one of the guests who were watching us, "is so the blind companion will know he has to stop and feel around with his foot for a change in the level of the terrain: a step up or a step down. That way, he won't stumble and hurt himself."

When I came to a set of stairs, I learned to Stop and Sit to give my companion a chance to get ready for climbing. After I had learned Forward, Right, Left, Haul Up and Stop, and Stop and Sit, Jack added a new element to the game. He tied a kerchief around his eyes. Then he picked up the harness handle and said, "Forward."

I cast him an anxious look over my shoulder. *Are you sure you want to play this game?* What did he think he was doing? His eyes were covered up. If he couldn't see, wouldn't he stumble or trip?

But Jack just repeated, "Forward," and I knew I had to obey.

And then it hit me: *this* was the game! I had

to take care of Jack and make sure he didn't hurt himself while he was wearing the blindfold. It was a little like herding a very confused herd of one. Jack's step was less assured with the blindfold on. I had to pull hard to keep him moving. He had some idea of where we were going and still gave me my directions, but I was the one who made sure we got there safely.

"This is how it will be to guide a real blind person," Jack said to a visitor who was watching. "The only difference is I can take off the blindfold. A blind person isn't that lucky. Kiss, here, will be serving as the blind person's eyes."

I wasn't at all sure what he meant by that, but whatever Jack said was the law as far as I was concerned. Mrs. Eustis might be the Lady Boss, but Jack was my Partner.

"Now, let's see if we can find our way to the

main house, Kiss," Jack said. "Forward."

We were standing in the big driveway turn-around. After we crossed the driveway and I Hauled Up and Stopped so Jack could feel his way up the curb, he said, "Forward."

I started to move forward, but then I hesitated. Somebody had rolled a cart piled with boxes smack into the middle of the path. I couldn't go forward without crashing us both into it. So I hesitated a moment, then guided Jack around the cart, even though he had told me to go straight.

"What's going on, Kiss?" Jack asked. I could hear in his voice that he was about to pop the leash. But I kept going.

Then Jack reached out and waved his arms around until he felt the cart. He broke out in a wide grin. "Oh, I get it!" he said. "There's an obstruction in our path. Good call, Kiss."

After that, I learned to go around anything that was in our path with no direction from Jack. Another time, I was guiding Jack along one of the garden paths when a child came zooming toward us on a bicycle.

"Forward," Jack said.

Wait a minute. If I went forward, Jack and I would collide with the bike rider. I made the decision. I disobeyed Jack and sat.

Jack popped the leash. "When I say 'Forward,' I mean *Forward,* Kiss," Jack said in that stern voice of his.

Still, I sat.

Then I guess Jack heard the bell go *ding-a-ling* and felt the whoosh of the bicycle as it passed in front of us.

Jack pulled up his blindfold and stared after the bike with wide eyes. "Now *that* is what's known

as Intelligent Disobedience," Jack said. "The most important trait a guide dog can have. Good girl!"

As you can imagine, I felt pretty good hearing that. Pleasing Jack meant everything to me.

Then one day, I let Jack down. We were passing under a chestnut tree when he bumped his head on a low-hanging branch. I didn't even notice it until he pulled up hard on my harness and said, "Ouch!" He rubbed his forehead. Then he said, "Forward!" He made us turn around and pass back underneath that same chestnut tree. I thought he would duck this time, since he knew about the low branch. But again, he bumped his head! He popped my leash. Jack had a mark on his forehead so it must have been sore. So to save his poor head, the next time he ordered me to walk beneath the chestnut tree, I guided him around the low-hanging branch.

"Good girl, Kiss!" Jack said.

From that day forth, whenever I wore the Working Harness, I knew to look not just at what *lay ahead* but also at what was *up above*. It wasn't enough that *I* could pass through safely. *Both* of us had to pass through without bumps or bruises. This was a complicated game, but it was fun!

One afternoon not long after the chestnut tree incident, Jack said to the Lady Boss, "Kiss has been doing great work. I think she's ready."

I *was* ready. I was ready to take care of Jack forever. Jack was the only Partner in the world for me. And he *needed* me. Without my guidance, he couldn't even make his way around Fortunate Fields without getting run over by a bicycle or bumping his head on a branch.

Jack and I were a Team.

BUDDY IS BORN

One morning, Jack came to the kennels early and brushed my coat until it shone.

I like a good brushing as much as the next dog, but what was the big occasion?

Oh, they've got something special in mind for you today, Gala told me.

Gala usually knew what she was talking about. So I wasn't all that surprised when, instead of buckling on my Working Harness, Jack marched me straight over to the Lady Boss's house.

Now, this was no regular house. It was a very fancy place. It even *smelled* fancy. Like lemons and cheese and fine meats and flowery perfume. As I trotted down the fragrant, carpeted halls, I held my head high and puffed out my chest with pride.

"Hello, Kiss," said the maid.

"Good day to you, Kiss," said the cook.

"Hello, Kiss," said George, the Lady Boss's husband.

"Good luck, Kiss," said the Lady Boss herself when she saw me.

Sorry, can't stop now, my look said to them. Normally, it would have been perfectly okay for me to do so. But Jack was in such an all-fired hurry I had to scramble to keep up with him. He brought me down a hallway to a closed door, where he said, "Stay, Kiss." Leaving me sitting outside, he opened the door and disappeared. I heard him speaking with someone on the other side of the door. What was going on?

Moments later, Jack came out of the room and left the door open.

"Here, girl!" someone inside the room said.

That usually meant me. I stood up and peered around the doorjamb.

It was a small room, considering that most of the rooms in the Lady Boss's house were huge. There was space enough for a bed, a chair, a chest, and a door leading to the place where people do their business. There was a stranger standing in the middle of the room. A man, not much older than a boy, was holding out his hand to me. In his hand was a big, juicy wad of raw meat.

I took a few steps into the room, my claws clicking on the polished wooden floors, and stared

at the man. He didn't stare back. He was staring at the air above my head. I took a few more steps forward—*click, click, click*—and sniffed at the meat.

"Go ahead and take it, girl," the man said in a soft, friendly voice.

Was this some sort of a game? I'd played Don't

Take Food from Strangers many times before. This was a stranger, and that was food in his hand. But it smelled so good! How was I supposed to play this? Well, I didn't have my Working Harness on, so I figured maybe it was okay just this once. I lifted my muzzle, and ever so daintily—I am nothing if not a lady—I took the wad of meat from his hand and ate it. Afterward, I licked my chops.

My, but that tasted good!

The stranger still held out his hand, so I took the hint and licked the meat juice off his fingers.

"Atta girl," said the man. Then he patted me with his meat-smelling hand.

That was when Jack reappeared. He said to the stranger, "This is your guide dog, Mr. Frank. Mr. Frank, say hello to Kiss."

What are you talking about, Jack? I'm your guide dog. I'm your Partner. We're a Team, you and I. You can't walk down the street without me.

The man knelt beside me and moved his hands all over my body. He even ran his fingers down the length of my tail.

"Kiss?" he said with a short laugh. "What kind of a sissy name is *that* for a dog? I can't call you Kiss. *Come here, Kiss! Sit, Kiss.* I'd be laughed off the streets of Nashville."

I didn't see what was so funny. Kiss was my name! *You don't see me laughing at* your *name, do you?*

Mr. Frank said, "From now on, you're going to be Buddy. Because that's exactly what you are. You're my partner and my guide and my good, good buddy." Mr. Frank wrapped his arms around my neck and hugged me.

Easy does it, Buster! This Mr. Frank had one fierce hug!

For once, Jack sounded a little unsure of himself. "Well," he said, "she's your dog, so I guess if you want to change her name, that's your privilege. It might take her a while to respond to Buddy. She's always been Kiss to us. She comes to Kiss."

"Well, she'll be coming to Buddy as of today," Mr. Frank said in a firm voice. "Right, Buddy?"

I looked up at him. He still wasn't returning my gaze. His eyes stared at the air over my head. That got me a little worried. I looked to Jack. *Really, Jack?*

Jack said, "You heard him, Kiss. You're Buddy from now on."

I sighed. So I guess I was kissing Kiss goodbye and saying hello to Buddy.

"Okay, Mr. Frank," said Jack. "Buddy's going to take good care of you, but that means you have to take good care of Buddy. I told you where the cans and the opener were earlier. Give her half a can twice a day. Make sure she gets plenty to drink. Brush her coat every day. And take her outside to do her business four times a day."

"Don't worry, Mr. Humphrey. I got the drill," said Mr. Frank. "Do you have the harness?" He reached out and groped around in the air every which way with his arms.

Jack carefully placed the harness in Mr. Frank's hands. He ran his fingers over it.

"Those are the buckles," Jack explained. "This is the hard handle. The handle is the secret to working with the dog. Through the handle, you'll be able to feel where she's moving and she'll be able to feel where you're moving. You hold it in your left hand at all times. Let's see if you can get the harness on her."

"Can't you do that?" Mr. Frank said with an

uneasy laugh. "You're the big-time dog expert."

"You're about to become one, too," said Jack.

"Starting now. Give it a try."

Mr. Frank groped around for me. I moved closer to make it easier. It took some doing for him to make sense of the harness and how it fit on my body. In the process, he stepped on my toes, squished my ears, and poked me in the eye. He wasn't very good at this game. But I was patient with him. Finally, he managed to buckle the harness on.

Jack checked it and loosened a buckle.

"All set? Okay, Buddy, let's see what you can do. Forward," said Mr. Frank.

Forward? Really, Mr. Frank? There was a wall in front of us.

And *that's* how my partnership with Morris Frank began.

Later that evening, after a long day of getting to know each other, Mr. Frank took me back to the small room. I had noticed that people light up the rooms of their houses at night, but this Mr. Frank stayed in the dark. In the dark, he took off my harness and hung it on the back of the chair. He opened a can and scooped out my food into a bowl. When he set the bowl down on the floor, he spilled a bit but didn't seem to notice. Food on the floor tastes just as good as food in a bowl, so that wasn't a problem. He set down a bowl of water, sloshing a lot of it onto the floor. I lapped up what was left in the bowl. Then I ate all the food. After that, I sat down and waited for Jack to come back and take me to the kennels. I was tired, but eager to get back to my pal Gala and tell her all about my day with Morris Frank.

I watched while Mr. Frank groped around in the dark. He took off his clothes and put on some lighter, softer ones. I had to keep my eye on him and shift myself around; otherwise he would have fallen over me as he moved from the chest to the bed. There was barely enough space in that room for the two of us. When he lifted the covers and climbed into the bed, he felt around for me.

"Where are you, Buddy?" he asked.

Here I am. I walked over and stood beside the bed. I panted loud enough so that he could locate me in the darkness.

"There you are!" He found my head and stroked my ears. "Down," he commanded.

I lay beside the bed. It didn't look as if I was going back to the kennels. I heaved a sigh.

"Good girl!" he said, running his hand along my back. "You're going to need your rest. Jack says today was just a warm-up. Tomorrow the *real* work starts. But I'm ready. Are you, girl?"

I'm always ready, but right then I was off duty.

Jack had left me my favorite rubber ball. The rule was I could chew it at night when my Working Harness was off. I found that it helped me unwind from a stressful day. And today had been plenty stressful. I rolled the ball between my paws and started to gnaw it.

Mr. Frank kept right on talking. He was a talker, this one. "It's you and me, girl, from here on in," he said. "Wait till they get a load of us back home in Nashville. Won't *they* be impressed? You know, girl, I was shipped here from America via American Express. Just like a package. They locked me in my cabin because they were afraid I'd hurt myself wandering around unsupervised. Can you imagine that? Treating a fellow like a prisoner, just because he can't see. But all that's over now. When I go home with you—my very own, honest-to-Betsy Seeing Eye dog—I'm traveling first-class, with the door unlocked. Like a respectable human being—right, Buddy, old girl?"

I looked up from my ball. My ears twitched at the sound of my new name.

"Who knows? With Mrs. Eustis's help, maybe we can open a school in America to train dogs like you and blind folks like me. And you're going to be with me every step of the way, Buddy, because I can't do it without you."

Morris Frank reached down and found my head again. Then he stroked my ears gently.

Maybe this Morris fellow was going to work out all right, after all. Still, I couldn't help myself. I missed spending all my time with Jack.

TRAINING MORRIS

Happily, in the days ahead, I saw as much of Jack as I did of Morris. It didn't take me long to understand why. Jack may have taught *me* how to play the guiding game, but Morris? He didn't have a clue how to play it. Still, if anyone was going to teach him, it would be Jack Humphrey.

"Fortunate Fields will be your training ground for the world beyond the gates of this estate," Jack said. "First of all, you'll need to know your way around this place backward and forward. I want you to have a complete mental picture of your surroundings."

"Sure thing," said Morris, "but I bet Buddy knows this place like the back of her paw."

"I don't think you understand," Jack said. "Buddy won't know which direction to go unless you tell her. You need to know where you're going first in order to direct her. Her job is to follow your directions and see that you get where you want to go safely and efficiently."

"Okay," said Morris, sounding a little less confident now. "So show me the lay of the land, Jack."

Jack started by leading Morris and me all around Fortunate Fields, telling him what everything looked like and where it was located compared to everything else: the driveway, the gardener's sheds, the bicycle racks, the garage for the horseless carriages, the garden with its many winding paths.

Jack wound up the tour beside the fountain in the middle of the garden. "All right, Mr. Frank, your first assignment is to find your way from here to the kitchen of Mrs. Eustis's house."

"That ought to be a cinch," said Morris. "Buddy and I can sniff our way there, right, girl?"

"The idea is to tell Buddy how to get there through the use of the basic commands," Jack said. "Yesterday, we went over the basic commands. Do you remember what they are?"

I knew those commands in my sleep. But Jack wasn't asking me. He was asking Morris.

"Piece of cake," said Morris. "There's Forward, Right, and Left."

"*And,*" Jack added, "if she hauls up and stops, it's for a very good reason. It might be a curb or some other change in the level of the footing. If she stops and sits, it's probably stairs or an obstruction she can't easily get around. Are you ready to go?"

"Where are *you* gonna be?" Morris asked.

"I'll be hovering somewhere nearby. Don't worry. I'll be watching," said Jack.

Jack walked away. But I didn't pay him any mind. I knew my job was to keep my attention on Morris and play the game with him.

"Let's see," Morris said under his breath. "If I remember, the path goes straight, and then there's a sharp right. Okay, Buddy. Forward." I walked the garden path in a straight line, the gravel crunching beneath our feet. Having Morris at the other end of the harness felt a lot different from Jack. To begin with, Morris walked slower. We had only gone a few steps and yet it felt like I was dragging a sled full of rocks. I came to the curb and Hauled Up and Stopped. But Morris wasn't paying him any attention. I could tell he had his mind on where he was *going* instead of where he *was.* That's why he didn't stop when I stopped. He walked right off the curb and stumbled.

"Buddy!" he yelled at me. "How could you let me do that?"

That was when Jack stepped in. "It's not Buddy's fault, Mr. Frank! Buddy was doing her job. She stopped. You weren't doing *your job,* which is to pay attention to what Buddy is doing on her end of the harness. Remember, that U-shaped harness is your link to Buddy. And Buddy is your link to the world. You should be able to feel through your hand when Buddy hauls up and stops, when she sits, when she turns. You have to pay close attention and follow her lead."

Jack made me walk and stop and walk and stop to give Morris a chance to know what it felt like. All the time, Morris was frowning. I could tell he didn't like being trained. And he especially didn't like being wrong.

After that, Morris paid careful attention as he

directed me to go left past the bicycle rack, right along the side of the garage, forward down the path between the lilacs, and left up to the back of Mrs. Eustis's house. There I Hauled Up and Sat at the foot of the stairs that led to the kitchen. Morris lifted his foot up onto the first step, following me. I led him up the rest of the steps. He opened the door, and we entered my favorite room of the house: the kitchen.

The cook turned from the stove and said, "Why, hello, Kiss! To what do we owe this honor?"

I sat and tried very hard not to moan at the many delicious smells wafting all around me.

"Her name is Buddy now," said Morris.

"Buddy, is it?" The cook looked at Morris and then at me. "Well, I guess I can get used to that if she can. I see that Buddy's doing a mighty good job of showing you around the place."

Just then, Jack arrived. "You made good time. Good job, Mr. Frank!" he said.

Morris grinned from ear to ear. Well, what do you know? Morris received praise when he played it right, just like us dogs.

Later that same day, Morris was directing me Forward. But, meanwhile, that wily Jack had gone and shut a gate that had been open earlier in the day. The closed gate loomed before me. What was a dog to do? I couldn't very well open it myself. And it was clear that Morris didn't know the gate was closed, because when I sat down in front of it, he said, "Forward!"

What choice did I have? I sat.

"I said 'Forward,' Buddy," Morris said.

When I continued to sit, Morris popped my leash. Still, I didn't move. That wasn't going to stop Morris, though. He barged ahead of me and banged his chin—*bonk*—against that hard metal gate.

"Ouch!" he said, staggering backward and rubbing his chin. Then he lashed out at me. "Why didn't you warn me, Buddy?"

Again, Jack came to my rescue. "Buddy *did* warn you, Morris. She stopped and sat. What did I tell you about Buddy stopping and sitting?"

"Yeah, yeah, yeah," Morris said. "It means she's sittin' for a reason. And if I didn't have such a thick skull, maybe that lesson would get through to me."

He laughed, then Jack laughed, and all three of us relaxed.

I couldn't help but think that what Morris needed to learn his lesson was for someone to pop his leash. But that wasn't going to happen anytime soon. Not unless he started wearing a harness.

That night in the dark of the little room, after

Morris had eaten and fed me, he let out a loud groan as he changed for bed. "I feel like an old man. I don't think I've ever been so tired in my life!"

You and me both.

Morris lay down on the bed and started talking. I stretched out on the floor with my head on my paws and listened.

"Boy, am I tired! I guess I'm not used to getting so much exercise." He heaved a huge sigh. "This is hard, Buddy. I knew it was going to be hard, but I never expected it to be *this* hard. I came here from the States so cocky, so ready to ace this thing, and now I'm not so sure." Morris trailed off, and soon he was asleep. I dropped off to sleep myself, without even chewing my ball, I was that tired.

Morris was up early the next morning, back to being a chatterbox. He spooned out my morning meal and did a pretty neat job of it, I must say. Then we were off to the training grounds. Didn't Morris want to eat? I guess he wanted to play more than he wanted to eat.

Bit by bit in the days to come, Morris and I came together as a Team. He began to understand how to use the harness and how to use me to move more safely.

Then, six days after Morris and I started working together, Jack said to us, "I think you two are ready to visit Vevey, the village down the hill."

"Look out, Vevey! Here we come!" Morris said.

The first few times we went to the quaint little alpine hamlet of Vevey, Jack came with us, and I can't say that I minded. To get to Vevey from Fortunate Fields, we had to take a cable car. Most of the passengers were used to seeing dogs riding to and from town. But this dog wasn't used to the cable car. It was noisy and crowded and smelled like boiling oil and smoke. I had to guide Morris up steep little steps and down a narrow aisle to a seat. Morris sat down hard. I sat in the aisle next to him. As the cable car crawled down the mountainside, Morris stroked my coat.

"You excited, Buddy?" Morris asked me.

I sat and looked straight ahead. *Alert? Yes. Excited? No.* Being excited wasn't part of the game. A German shepherd remained calm and composed at all times.

"I still wish she could show a little more affection now and then," Morris said to Jack.

"How many times do I have to tell you, Morris? She's not a pet. She's a highly intelligent trained animal whose job is to look after you. Who knows, maybe someday she might even save your life."

Morris didn't say anything, but his forehead was wrinkled and I could tell he was thinking really hard.

A CLOSE CALL

The streets of Vevey were a challenge, even for a smart dog like me. They were steep and twisty, and the curbs were high. The Forward command didn't mean straight ahead, as Jack explained to us, so much as it meant follow the sidewalk and try not to fall off the curb. I tried very hard to keep Morris on the sidewalk, but he was forever falling off those very high curbs and stumbling into the street. This made me feel bad, like I wasn't doing my job properly. Like I said, it was a challenge. But challenges exist to be overcome, as every good German shepherd knows.

Vevey was a noisy place, too. The only sounds to be heard in Fortunate Fields were the birds and the bees and the Lady Boss's man playing the piano. Here there were bells clanging and music blaring and horns honking and people talking and shouting and laughing.

And the scents! I don't think I've ever picked up so many different scents in one place. There were fresh breads from the bakery and juicy meats from the butcher. There were stinky cabbages and musky carrots from the greengrocer and sweet flowers from the flower stalls and sweating horses *everywhere* with their heavy, clip-clopping hooves and their hot, huffing breath. There were horseless carriages, too, rumbling and coughing and sputtering around every corner like metal monsters on wheels belching smoke. But I tuned out all of these things and kept my focus on Morris and where he was going.

While I did this, there were other distractions of a more challenging nature. There were children with sticky fingers thrusting flaky pastries and juicy sausages in my face, all wanting to share with me.

Was I tempted to taste their offerings?

Did I want nothing more than to gobble up their treats and lick their fingers clean?

Of course! But resisting these temptations was one of the objects of the game. Morris, to his credit, did his best to make it easier for me.

"Please don't try to feed my dog," he would say as nicely as he could. "She's not supposed to eat while she's working."

A group of sweet-smelling ladies gathered

round me while we waited on the curb for a horse-less carriage to chug past. The ladies cooed and made a big fuss over me.

"She looks so fierce and serious, doesn't she?" one of the ladies said.

"I think she looks noble," another lady gushed.

"She looks kind of unfriendly to me," a third muttered. "Does she bite?"

"Oh, no! My dog would never bite. She's very

polite," Morris said. "She's a highly intelligent animal, trained by experts to guide me. She's not your typical Fido, are you, Buddy?"

I had no time for their idle chitchat, however. I had much more important things to do. Like looking straight ahead at the street and waiting for the horseless carriage to move past so we could be on our way.

Morris and I spent all day walking around that

village. As the hours wore on, I could feel Morris starting to drag his feet. I could tell that he was exhausted. I was pretty tuckered out myself. It was hard work guiding him up and down those steep streets.

After we had gotten out of the cable car and were almost home, we came to a set of stone stairs. That morning, when I had stopped at the bottom, Morris had known to climb up the steps. That evening, however, when I stopped and sat down at the top, it was another story. Morris must have forgotten about the stairs, or maybe he was in a hurry to get home. For whatever reason, he ignored my signal and tumbled headlong down the stairs.

I whimpered and tucked in my tail. Morris lay sprawled at the bottom. His shirt had come untucked, and he looked a proper mess. This time, he didn't blame me. He blamed Jack, who had been

62

following behind us. "You *knew* those stairs were there! Yet you *deliberately* let me fall," he said in a sharp voice.

"Buddy tried to tell you to stop but you ignored her, and this is what happens when you don't pay attention to your guide dog," Jack said.

Poor Morris! Jack was one tough customer!

Morris gritted his teeth. I could tell he wanted to say something even sharper to Jack, but instead he sat up and groped around for his hat. He dusted it off and clapped it back on his head. By the time he had climbed to his feet and reached out for the harness, I was down at the bottom of the stairs, waiting to take him home.

Later, in the little room, Morris lay on the bed and I stretched out on the floor beside him, like we always did. But tonight, I could tell from the sound of his voice that he was feeling discouraged.

"My feet hurt, my left arm aches, and my legs are covered with bruises and scratches. I could have broken my neck falling down those stairs. I don't know how much more of this I can take. Maybe I'm not cut out to have a guide dog. Maybe I don't deserve to be anything more than a package in the baggage compartment. I'm going to Mrs. Eustis first thing tomorrow and telling her to forget about starting a school for The Seeing Eye. I'm not the right man for the job."

Morris stopped talking, and soon I heard a wet, sniffling sound. The whole bed was shaking.

Something was wrong with Morris!

In a flash, I leapt up onto the bed, even though I knew it wasn't my place. I found Morris curled up tight, with his face turned to the wall, his shoulders trembling. I climbed over him and nosed around for his face. When I finally found it, I discovered that it was all wet. I started licking it. That's what my mother used to do for me when I needed a little pick-me-up. Now I had to do the same for Morris.

Come on, Morris, old pal, cheer up. Things will get better. You'll see.

Morris rolled onto his back and hugged me to his chest. "Oh, Buddy! You understand, don't you? You're probably the only one in the world who does. Thank you, girl! That's just what I needed."

I waited on the bed until I was sure that he had fallen asleep. Then I returned to my place on the floor.

In the morning, just to make sure Morris was all right, I jumped up onto the bed again and licked his face until he stirred and woke up.

He laughed and hugged me. "I tell you, I can't

think of a friendlier wake-up call, Buddy!" he said.

Morris seemed so happy that I decided to wake him up every morning with a couple of nice, wet kisses. He always thanked me but, truth to tell, it was my pleasure. His face tasted good.

I don't know whether it was the morning kisses or plenty of hard work and practice (or maybe a combination), but in no time, we both knew our way around the village of Vevey. Even though Jack still came with us, he had taken to falling so far back behind us that, after a while, we both forgot he was even there. The less we heard from Jack on these trips, the more we knew we were playing the game right.

Late one afternoon, Morris and I were making our way up the street toward home when I heard a loud scrambling of horse hooves somewhere ahead of us in the road. Then two giant horses dragging their wagon harness came careening around the corner.

People screamed and ran. A woman picked up her child and hid behind a tree.

"What's all the commotion, Buddy?" Morris called out.

All I knew was that those wild-eyed horses were headed right for us!

Think, Buddy, think! To the right, the mountain dropped off into space. To the left, there was a steep, grassy slope. I knew I had to act fast. I dragged Morris off the road. He scrambled after me as I ran up the slope. When I had led Morris as far up as I could go, I stopped and watched as the horses tore past and disappeared around the bend.

Good riddance to bad horses!

Morris and I stood there, both of us panting, Morris sweating. Moments later, Jack caught up with us. He took off his hat and swabbed his forehead with a hanky.

"That was the most *amazing* thing I have ever seen! Two horses broke loose from their carriage and bolted. I thought you were going to get trampled for sure. Morris, Buddy saved your life!"

"Good girl, Buddy!" Morris got down and hugged me hard. This time, I didn't mind so much. In fact, you might say that I needed the hug. That had been a pretty close call.

Later, Morris showed his appreciation properly. As a side dish to my usual dinner, he got the cook to give me a nice hefty marrow bone to chew on. The bone was chewy, and the marrow was as smooth as cream! I don't think I have ever tasted anything so delicious in my life. That Morris! He sure knew the way to a dog's heart.

HIPPITY-HOP TO THE BARBERSHOP

One morning, Morris woke up and said, "My hair is getting as long and shaggy as yours, Buddy. I could use a good haircut today. Let's go find Jack and see if he can help us."

After Morris fed me, he strapped on my Working Harness and we went looking for Jack. He was usually somewhere in the big house. We went to the Lady Boss's office first.

The Lady Boss was sitting at her desk, writing.

I looked around the room, but Jack wasn't there.

I sat in the doorway and Morris cleared his throat. "Is that you, Mrs. Eustis? Good morning."

The Lady Boss looked up from her work. "Good morning, Mr. Frank. Good morning, Buddy."

I thumped my tail once on the floor.

"Is Jack here?" Morris asked.

"No, he's not," she said. "He's over in the kennels, working with some dogs. What can I do for you?"

"I need a haircut," Morris said.

"I can see that," the Lady Boss said with a smile.

Morris waited, then said, "Somebody needs to take me to town to the barbershop."

The Lady Boss set down her pen on her desk. "Mr. Frank, no one needs to take you anywhere," she said. "You can go to the barbershop on your own. You have got everything you need to be completely independent at the end of that harness."

I looked up at Morris. I could see him working this out. Then a wide grin spread across his face. "Sure thing!" he said. "Come on, Buddy, you and me are going to town on our own. Forward."

I must admit, it felt a little strange passing through the gates of Fortunate Fields without Jack. But it wasn't as if I hadn't made this trip many times before. We climbed the stone steps and waited for the cable car. When the cable car came, I led Morris up the steps, just like I always did.

"Good morning, Mr. Frank. Good morning, Buddy," the cable car driver said.

"Good morning, Dieter," Morris said.

"Is Jack coming?" Dieter asked.

"Not today," said Morris, grinning. "Today we're on our own."

When we got to the village, Morris said, "I bet you're wondering if I know the way to the barbershop, eh, girl? Don't worry. We'll just follow our noses until we pick up the scent of bay rum and hair oil, and then we'll know we're headed in the right direction."

We passed the baker and the butcher and the greengrocer and the flower stall, sniffing all the way. Then Morris stopped and tapped his nose. I sniffed, too. It smelled sharp and spicy.

"The barbershop should be over there somewhere, Buddy," he said, pointing to the right.

I led him a few paces. Morris stopped, so I stopped. The sharp, spicy scent was stronger.

We were standing in front of a shop with a big window and a striped pole in front. *This must be the barbershop.* Through the window I saw a man leaning back in a strange metal chair. He had a white sheet draped over his body and white foam all over his face. Another man in a white coat stood behind that man and scraped off the foam with a shiny stick. *This must be the barber.*

"This is the barbershop, Buddy," Morris said. "This is where I need to be."

I led him over to the door. Morris felt around for the handle and pushed open the door. We walked in. It was warm and steamy and spicy-smelling inside the shop.

I stopped in the middle of the floor. I didn't want to get in the way of the man in the white coat.

"I need a haircut," Morris said.

The barber wiped the shiny stick on his sleeve and said, "I am happy to help. But I'm afraid that your dog will have to wait outside. There are no dogs allowed in my shop."

"Ah, but, good sir, this is no ordinary dog," Morris explained politely. "This dog is my Seeing Eye. I'm blind, and she helps guide me. Her name is Buddy. I assure you she is very well mannered. She has to be because wherever I go, she goes, too."

The barber nodded and thought about this. "All right, then. I guess we can make an exception this once. Please take a seat right here and I'll be with you in a moment."

The man pointed to the empty chair nearest the window. So I led Morris over to it. Morris had no trouble finding his way into the seat. I sat next to the chair so that my harness was within easy reach of Morris's left hand.

Soon the barber finished cutting the hair of the man in the chair next to us, removed the white sheet, and shook it out. The clean-shaven man rose from the chair, slapped some money into the barber's hand, and went whistling out the door.

Then the barber turned to Morris. He spread a fresh white sheet over Morris until only his head showed. Then he got a pair of shiny, snippy things and started to cut Morris's hair. Clumps of it drifted down over my head. A couple got up my nose and I sneezed.

"Gesundheit!" said the barber as he snipped.

When the barber went to cut the hair on the left side of Morris's head, I moved out of his way and waited until he was done before I moved back. I didn't want him to trip over me with those sharp, shiny, snippy things in his hand.

"That's a pretty smart dog you have," the barber said to Morris as the snippy things went *snip-snip-snip*.

"She's the best," Morris said. "She's been trained to guide me. Before I got her, I was completely

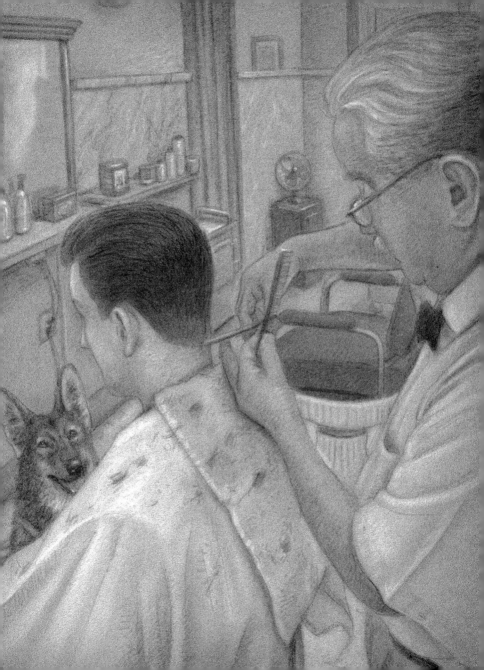

dependent on people to take me wherever I needed to go. But with Buddy, I can go anywhere and do anything."

"My grandmamma could have used one of those," the barber said. "She was blind and we grandkids had to lead her around the village."

"I don't need anyone to lead me but Buddy. I'm taking her back to the States and we're going to open a Seeing Eye school."

"Good luck to you." The barber set down the snippy things and picked up another tool. It reminded me of the sheep shearers. The barber used it to trim the hair on Morris's neck. Morris didn't mind half as much as the sheep had.

When the barber was finished with Morris, he pulled off the white sheet. Morris took out his wallet and gave the man money.

Out on the street, Morris asked me, "How do I look, Buddy? Did the barber do a good job?"

Don't ask me, Morris. I'm a dog.

But the truth was, he looked neater—and a whole lot happier. On the way to the cable car station, Morris's step was so light! I hardly had to pull him at all. He couldn't stop talking about his haircut and how happy he was to be with me in the village all by himself. I was happy, too, but I was busy, keeping a sharp eye out for anything unexpected, like runaway horses.

When we got back to Fortunate Fields, Morris marched us right into the big house to the Lady Boss's office. The Lady Boss wasn't there, but we found her in the big living room.

She looked up when we came in. "Don't you look handsome," she said.

"You're looking at a free man, Mrs. Eustis!" Morris said. "I just went and got myself a haircut without a single hitch. From now on, I can go anywhere and do *anything*. I'm ready to go back to the States and show everyone that sightless people can be independent. I admit that over the last few weeks, I've had my doubts. But now I know we can do it, Mrs. Eustis. I *know* we can open this school and make this precious freedom available to other people like me."

There was water running down Morris's cheeks but he was laughing, too. People were such a puzzle sometimes.

"I don't mean to dampen your enthusiasm," said the Lady Boss, "but you've got your work cut out for you. People will need to be convinced. You and Buddy will have to demonstrate to all those doubters that the Seeing Eye system really works."

"We can do it. I know we can!" Morris said. "Buddy and I will show them how we can walk down the street like anybody else."

"Bear in mind that the streets in America are a lot busier than the ones in our sleepy little hamlet."

"I know they are. But Buddy and I can handle it, can't we, girl?" Morris said.

You bet we can. I thumped my tail on the floor.

"Many eyes will be on you, and they'll all be waiting for you to stumble," the Lady Boss said.

"So what if I fall?" Morris said. "I'll get up and dust myself off. I'm no quitter."

"The other thing you're going to have to do is work to change the laws."

"What laws?"

"There are laws in America and throughout the

world," the Lady Boss said, "that don't allow dogs into restaurants, offices, train stations, and other public places."

"I can do it, Mrs. Eustis. We—Buddy and I—can do it," said Morris.

"Well, if you can," said the Lady Boss, "I'll give you ten thousand dollars to start your new school."

"Mrs. Eustis, you have got yourself a deal!" Morris said. "When do we sail for the good old US of A?"

MAIDEN VOYAGE

After Morris and I had said our farewells to Jack and Gala, the Lady Boss came to see us off at the little train station in Vevey. She got down on her knees and gave me a big hug. Her face was wet, and I was tempted to lick her but I didn't. After all, she was the Lady Boss. It wouldn't have been right.

"You take good care of Morris, now," she whispered in my ear.

I gazed across the lake at the snowcapped

mountains in the distance, then looked back at her. *Guiding Morris is my entire life.*

The Lady Boss pulled back and stared at me. "Just look at you, you noble creature! Off to do Great Things in the world. This is a proud day for me."

I puffed out my chest. It was a proud day for me, too, although I had no idea what awaited me.

The next few hours were difficult for both Morris and me. First we rode on one train; then we got out and looked for another. Morris had to stop and ask for directions, and then he gave the directions to me. The trains all looked alike. They were lined up on the tracks in a row inside a vast train station. The trains were chuffing and puffing steam. There were crowds of people, rushing in all directions. And there were Morris and me, in the middle of all these people in the vast station. We

got mixed up and lost, and Morris had to stop two
more people before we got the correct directions.

When we finally climbed on the second train
and found our seats in the tiny compartment, the
conductor came and tried to take me away from
Morris. He wanted me to ride in the baggage car.
But Morris told the man that I, Buddy, was no

piece of baggage. We, Morris and Buddy, had to stay together.

You tell them, Morris!

"We're a team," Morris said. His voice sounded high and nervous and I was a little worried he might get angry. Morris had a temper if he was pushed too far.

"Then may I suggest, sir, that you ride in the baggage car with your dog," the conductor said.

"No, sir," said Morris, shaking his head firmly. "That's not going to happen."

Grumbling, the conductor went away and came back a few minutes later with a policeman. Now both the conductor and the policeman were yelling at Morris. Morris yelled back. People in the other compartments heard the commotion and came to see what it was all about. They gathered in the hall outside our compartment.

"This dog is special," Morris told the train conductor and the policeman. "I need her with me because I can't see without her."

"Let the dog stay!" the people in the hallway said.

In the end, the conductor and the policeman threw up their hands and let Morris and me stay with the rest of the passengers. They cheered and patted me. As always, I remained calm and unruffled, but I was very relieved that the yelling had stopped. Poor Morris was so tired from arguing that he fell asleep as soon as the train started moving. I dozed but woke up every few minutes to make sure Morris was okay. He was still asleep when the train pulled into the final station, so I had to wake him up with a firm paw on his knee.

When we stepped off the train, I saw strange, big white birds. They were wheeling and cawing and diving in the air above water. I knew all about water, of course—the water in my bowl, in the pond on the sheep farm, and in mountain lakes. But this was more water in one place than I had ever seen. It seemed to stretch on forever. My nose twitched. I smelled fish and salt and wind.

"Smell that? That's the sea, Buddy. You're going to be smelling that a lot from now on. Let's go find our steamship," he said.

A man with a cap went ahead of us, carrying Morris's bags in his arms. He led us straight to our ship. It floated on the water, rising up higher and bigger than any building I had ever seen. It was like a huge, floating village.

"This is going to be our home for the next week," Morris said.

A home that floated on the water? It looked like I had my work cut out for me. What if Morris fell off the side of the ship into the water? I couldn't let that happen. I had to be vigilant and alert to new dangers.

I followed the man with Morris's bags up a steep, narrow wooden ramp. Morris held on to the rail with one hand and to my harness with the other. I had to pull hard because Morris was having trouble keeping his balance. It was hard enough staying upright with four legs. Morris must have found it a real challenge with only two. Below the steep walkway lay the water, black and oily and smelling strongly of fish. The ramp creaked and moved up and down. The whole ship moved up and down.

Morris staggered to the top. A man in a white suit and a black hat with a shiny bill was waiting for us.

"Welcome aboard. I'm the captain of this

vessel. Mrs. Eustis told us to expect you. This must be Buddy, the wonder dog. My crewman will show you to your cabin. It's on the upper-deck level. We thought Buddy might have a little trouble climbing up and down ladders. Enjoy the voyage. And please let me know if there's anything you need."

"Gee, thanks, Captain," said Morris. "Did you hear that, Buddy?" he asked as we followed the crewman along the deck. "Nobody's treating us like baggage now."

I didn't pay Morris much mind. The floor was tipping this way and that. I had to concentrate to keep us moving in a straight line. There was a wire railing on one side, where people leaned over and waved to their friends standing below on the dock. Some of the people stopped waving and turned to look as we passed by.

A woman with curly hair pointed at me and said, "Oh, look! A dog on board!"

"Isn't he beautiful?" a woman with black hair said.

Who are you calling a he?

"It's a girl, silly, not a boy," Curly Hair told her.

"Hey, isn't that the famous Seeing Eye dog I read about in a magazine?" a bearded man said.

"You got it," Morris said. "This is Buddy."

"Hey, Buddy, welcome aboard," Beard Man said. "Be seeing you in the dining room."

We followed the crewman to a room that was even smaller and cozier than the one we had shared in Switzerland. This one had a high, narrow bed that was bolted to the wall and a window that was round.

"I guess your dog is rooming with you," the crewman said.

"That's the plan. This old girl sticks to me like glue," said Morris.

"I'm sorry, but I don't think there's room in the bunk for you and your dog both," said the crewman.

"That's okay," Morris told him. "Buddy sleeps on the floor next to the bed. So long as she's within arm's reach, we're okay."

The man showed Morris where to put away his clothes and where to do his business. Before he left, Morris asked him to bring a pitcher of water. After that, he went away and left us to ourselves.

I was sitting, watching Morris put his clothes away, when suddenly there was a loud noise. It shook the entire ship. I stood up.

What was that?

Morris reached out and patted my head. "Don't worry, girl. That sound means the ship is putting out to sea. Your maiden voyage is about to begin."

When Morris had finished unpacking his clothes, he unpacked my food and my bowls. I must say, I had worked up quite an appetite finding my way around all those train stations. Morris scooped out my food and put the bowl down on the floor beneath the round window. And do you know what? He didn't even spill any. I thought he was doing a pretty good job, considering that all of this must have been as new and strange to him as it was to me.

After I had eaten my dinner, we followed our noses out of the cabin and along the deck until we came to a room bigger than any of the rooms at the Lady Boss's house, where the rooms were mighty spacious. There must have been a hundred round tables, each filled with people talking and laughing and shouting and eating and drinking and clanking their silverware against their plates. Among the crowd, I saw the captain and the crewmen and also the friendly passengers who had spoken to Morris earlier.

"Something smells delicious!" Morris said, lifting his nose in the air.

I know just what you mean.

Curly Hair rose from her chair and crossed to us. "Won't you join our table?" she asked.

"Oh, hello again," Morris said, turning to Curly Hair. "I remember you from on deck. Sure thing! I'd love to."

We followed her over to where she sat with Beard Man and Black Hair. Curly Hair took Morris's other hand and led him to the empty chair next to hers. Morris sat down. I sat down next to Morris's chair. Black Hair was seated on the other side of me.

"Hey, puppy dog!" she said.

Hey, yourself. It had been a long time since anyone had called me that. She held out her hand to me. She was holding a savory piece of meat. *Oh, my!* But there was no tempting this German shepherd. I just looked at that meat as if it were a small brown stone.

The woman frowned and said, "What's the matter, puppy dog? Filet mignon not good enough for you?"

Morris turned to her. "Buddy's already had her dinner. And she's not supposed to accept food while she's on duty. Thanks, though."

"You're pretty strict with her," Curly Hair said. "Doesn't Buddy ever get to have any fun?"

"At night, when her harness is off, she gets to relax," Morris said. "She has a toy ball that she chews."

"Well, whoop-de-doo for her," Black Hair said. "My dog, Rex, gets to run around and chase squirrels for kicks."

"Ah, but Rex isn't a highly trained animal with an important job to do," Morris said.

"Good point," said Black Hair.

"On the voyage over to Europe," Morris said, "I didn't have Buddy. The crew locked me in my cabin because they didn't want me falling over the rail and into the sea. I spent the entire voyage cooped up. This time, I'm traveling in style, thanks to Buddy."

Black Hair patted my head and said, "Good going, Buddy."

I do my best.

Morris laughed and chatted while he ate with his new friends. Except for the day he had gotten his hair cut, I had never seen him so happy.

The days that followed were pleasant except for when the sea was choppy. Then people appeared on deck wrapped in their coats looking a little green. Some of them leaned over the rail and threw up their meals into the sea. But the lurching deck didn't bother me.

You might be wondering where I did my business. Four times a day, Morris laid out some newspaper on the deck. I went on the newspaper. Then Morris wrapped up the newspaper and gave it to the nearest crewman, who took it away.

Everyone on board knew me by name. They called to me whenever they saw me. The captain had taken a special liking to me. Morris often ate at his table. One day, he invited Morris and me to visit him in the wheel room. From the wheel room the captain ran the entire ship.

"You and I have a lot in common," the captain

said to me. "I make sure the ship sails safely. You make sure it's Morris who moves safely, isn't that right, Captain Buddy?"

Every time he saw me after that, he raised his hand to his head and called me Captain Buddy.

On the last day of the voyage, after Morris had packed his clothes and my bowls, he directed me to a place on the ship called the business office.

"I need to switch my Swiss francs for good old US dollars," Morris told the man sitting at the desk in the business office.

Morris gave the man all the money in his wallet. The man counted it out, and then counted out a new stack of money for Morris. Morris put the new money into his wallet, then wedged the wallet in his back pocket. Usually, he patted his pocket after he put away his wallet, but this time, he didn't. And the wallet fell on the floor behind him. I looked up to see whether Morris had noticed, but he hadn't. So I bent down and picked up the wallet in my mouth. I lifted it toward his free hand, but Morris had already commanded me to move forward. With the wallet in my mouth, I led Morris back to our cabin.

When we got there, Morris took off my Working Harness. Still, he didn't notice the wallet in my mouth. He said, "I'm bushed from all that packing. Think I'll take me a little lie-down before we put into port." He lay down on the bunk with a weary groan.

Instead of stretching out next to the bunk like I usually did, I jumped up and rested my forepaws on the bunk. I still had the wallet in my mouth. It was getting kind of soggy from my drool, but there was nothing I could do about that.

"Hey, Buddy," Morris said drowsily when he

felt my weight pressing down on the mattress.

Excuse me. I tapped Morris with my paw and thrust the wallet toward him.

Morris patted my paw. "Leave me alone, Buddy. I told you, I'm tired," he said. He settled himself back on the pillow.

You don't get it, do you? Again, I tapped Morris with my paw.

"Stop it, Buddy! What's *with* you, anyway?" he said.

Finally, I opened my mouth and dropped the wallet on his chest. *I'll tell you what's with me. Your wallet!*

Morris quickly reached out and grabbed the wallet. He sat up with a start and slapped his head. "Holy Toledo—I must have dropped it! Buddy, you brilliant dog! I love you! You're worth more to me than the whole United States Mint."

Morris wrapped his arms around me and hugged me so hard my tongue hung out. It wasn't quite as satisfying as a marrow bone, but it was nice to be appreciated.

8

THE WIDEST STREET IN THE WORLD

Morris and I stood at the deck rail as the steamship approached our destination. It was a city on the water where buildings were packed in close together, rising so high that some of them seemed to scrape the sky. The streets between the buildings were packed with vehicles. This city was bigger and noisier and busier than any I had ever known. The ship rose and fell and rubbed against the side of the dock. Crewmen tossed down lines and ran along the deck shouting to each other. I did my best to keep Morris out of their way.

Down below, a huge crowd of people pushed and shoved, giving off a dull roar. A bunch of men worked their way through the crush of people to the bottom of the wooden ramp as I led Morris down into the thick of the crowd.

"There he is! That's him! He's got the dog with him!" one of the men shouted as he pointed at Morris and me.

"Welcome to the Port of New York!" another of the men said.

"Don't mind them," Morris said to me. "They're reporters, hungry for a story. We'll give them something juicy to write about, won't we, girl?"

The reporters lifted boxes to their faces and the boxes exploded in bursts of bright light. The light hurt my eyes. For a few moments, all I could see were spots. I blinked until my sight came back. The next time one of those boxes exploded, I knew enough to look away.

"Hey, mister!" a reporter with a white hat called out. "Is it true your guide dog can take you anywhere?"

Morris turned his head toward White Hat and grinned. "She sure can, and we'd be happy to prove it to you cynical members of the press."

The reporters put their heads together and carried on a conversation.

One man wearing a black hat backed away from the others. "I don't want any part in this," he said. "You gents won't be happy until you get them both killed!"

"Hey, we want proof and this is proof!" White Hat said. Then he said to Morris, "All right. You say your dog can take you anywhere. How about you let Wonder Dog take you across West Street? It just happens to be right here in front of you."

"Right here? Swell. No problem," Morris said. "Buddy crosses streets all the time, don't you, girl?"

The street in front of us had to have been wider than all the streets in Vevey combined. It was teeming with horseless carriages and trucks and carts and cable cars and pushcarts and teams of horses pulling heavy loads. But as far as Morris was concerned, this was an easy game for us to play.

"Forward!" Morris said.

I took a deep breath, then started to walk across the street. I hadn't gotten more than a few steps when I stopped and sat down.

"Hey, why is she sitting down?" one of the reporters shouted.

I was sitting down because if I had continued moving forward, I would have gotten both Morris and me run over by a horseless carriage! Instead, it whizzed past us, inches from our noses.

The driver leaned out of his window and shouted at us, "Are you crazy, or are you *trying* to get yourself killed?"

Don't look at me. This wasn't my idea.

"Wait up!" Black Hat dodged a bicycle and two horseless carriages to catch up with us. "That driver's right. This is a bad idea. Let me guide you back to the curb. We'll find you a safer street to cross."

But Morris shook his head firmly. "Nothing doing. This is the street we said we'd cross, and we're going to cross it, right, Buddy? Forward."

The road ahead was clear for now so I stood and continued on our way, Black Hat staying with us. This time, I managed to get us across two lanes of traffic before a huge truck came at us. I sat down. Morris stopped. As the truck banged past,

Morris leaned back and said, "Whew! That was a close one, wasn't it?"

Tell me about it!

I waited while a stream of horseless carriages followed in the wake of the truck. When I saw an opening, I stood up and moved us forward through it. Had I been on my own, I probably would have run across the street, weaving in and out of traffic, but I was guiding Morris so I couldn't take any chances. I stopped before some train tracks. I heard a bell and, moments later, a cable car ran past us. As soon as it was gone, I stood up and moved again.

Would this street never end?

"Hey, puppy dog!" one of the reporters hollered across the traffic. "Can you fetch?"

Did that fellow think he could turn my head? Didn't he know I was a working dog?

"This street has the worst traffic in New York,"

said Black Hat. "There must be fifteen lanes of the most unruly traffic anywhere on earth. Anyone who crosses it, even a sighted person, takes their life into their own hands."

Morris laughed nervously.

Four more times I sat and let vehicles pass before I would take Morris any farther. Once, I had to go back the way I came because it didn't seem safe. Finally, we got to the far curb. I stopped. Morris stepped up. We had just crossed the widest street in the world.

The reporters and all the people on the other side of the street who had been watching us leapt into the air and burst into loud cheers and applause.

"I guess Buddy showed us," Black Hat said.

"Did you hear that, girl?" Morris said to me. "I think you passed the test . . . with flying colors."

I might have passed the test, but deep down I was a nervous wreck. How did anyone *survive* in a city like this?

Later that day, Morris had me take him to a place called the telegraph office. In the office, there was a man with a visor sitting at a desk. He was making a steady tapping noise with his finger. He stopped tapping when he saw Morris and me come in.

"What can I do for you?" he asked.

"I need to send a message to a friend in Switzerland," Morris told the man. He gave the man the Lady Boss's address at Fortunate Fields.

"What's the message?" the man asked.

"The message," Morris said, leaning over the desk, "is 'SUCCESS!'"

The man tapped a few times. Then he stopped and seemed to be waiting for Morris to say more.

"That's it?" he asked.

"That's *it*? Believe me, mister, that's just about
everything!" Morris said.

The street games didn't stop there. From New
York, Morris took us to a place called Philadelphia,

where reporters met us in a train station so vast birds roosted near its ceiling. The reporters there also challenged us to cross their busiest street. While this street was not anywhere near as wide and busy as West Street, I still had my work cut out for me.

I was just getting used to Philadelphia when Morris took us on the train to a place called Cincinnati, where there were more reporters to charm and more bustling streets to cross.

In each city, Morris would slap the newspaper. "They tell me we made the front page. You're a big star, Buddy. You're famous."

I didn't really understand what Morris was talking about. All I knew was that these street-crossing games stressed me and made me tired. While I was playing them, I gave them—and Morris—my undivided attention. But at the end of each day, after Morris had climbed into his bed—in a strange new room every night—I would flop down on the floor. Who had the energy to chew a ball?

At night, I even *dreamed* of crossing crowded streets. Each day, I wondered, when would our journey end? I wanted to take Morris home, wherever that was.

9

THE SEEING EYE

When Morris and I finally got to Nashville, Tennessee, I was disappointed at first. While Switzerland was cool and bracing, Nashville was hot and steamy. Morris went around with his jacket off and his shirtsleeves rolled up, but there wasn't much I could do about my heavy coat. I panted a great deal and I found that I was thirsty all the time. Morris must have known how it was for me because he kept my bowl filled with cold water.

Morris knew the streets of Nashville backward and forward, and he knew the people, too. Those people he didn't know knew us from all the newspaper stories. We went out every day to send a telegram to the Lady Boss. Believe it or not, we still hadn't heard back from her. Meanwhile, Morris got lots of letters from strangers, which friends read to him. They were from blind people who had learned about us from stories in the newspapers. They all wanted dogs like me. They all wanted to be independent, like Morris. Morris wrote the same message back to all of them: "Soon, with the help of Mrs. Dorothy Eustis, I hope to open a school, the first school of its kind."

Morris continued to wait for word from the Lady Boss. Every day that he didn't get a letter from her, he grew more worried. He began to pace. When he paced without holding on to my handle, I worried. What if he tripped or bumped into something? I guess Morris and I were each worried, in our own ways.

"Where is she, girl?" Morris asked me. "Why hasn't she answered me or come through with our money?"

What did I know? The Lady Boss had always been a mystery to me.

While Morris waited, he tried to keep busy. We went to look at empty buildings that might make good dog kennels. Morris asked my opinion. I was unimpressed. None of them compared to our wonderful kennels at Fortunate Fields. We went to the homes of strangers who had dogs that they thought might make good guides. Some of them had promise. They were friendly but calm and smart. Others, however, were simply not cut out for it. I told one golden retriever, *I'm sorry, but you're too silly and bouncy to be a guide dog.*

Finally, Morris got a letter from Switzerland. The Lady Boss apologized and said that she had been having trouble finding people who knew how to train guide dogs. My old friend Jack did not want to work in the new school. There were other things he wanted to do, although I couldn't imagine what those things might be. What could be better than training more guide dogs like me? Eventually, I guess Jack saw the light.

One day, there was a knock on Morris's door. There was Jack, the Lady Boss, a strange girl, and two German shepherds.

A lot of handshaking and backslapping and hugging went on. Jack looked down at me and said, "Hello, Buddy, my old friend. It's good to see you again."

He scratched the scruff of my neck like he

used to. Then he said, "Buddy, I want you to meet Adelaide. Adelaide's all right. She's been learning how to train guide dogs. Maybe you can give her a tip or two."

Adelaide smiled at me. "You've been doing good work, Buddy. You're a very special dog. I read all about you in the *Saturday Evening Post.*"

But I wasn't paying all that much attention to Adelaide. My eyes were on my old friend from Fortunate Fields, Gala. Gala had come to America, along with another German shepherd.

Long time no see, I said to Gala.

We've missed you back at the kennels, said Gala. *I've been busy training, and now they think I'm ready to guide. They think Tartar is ready, too.*

Tartar was a handsome male German shepherd with touches of silver in his chest and tail. But his tongue hung out halfway to the floor.

Jeez! Tartar said. *It's as hot as blazes in this place. How can you* stand *it?*

It's Morris's hometown, so I have to make the best of it, I told him. *You should have been here a month ago. It was even hotter. You dogs had better get used to the fact that you're not in Switzerland anymore.*

The people all sat down in Morris's living room. They drank from tall glasses that tinkled with ice and ate cookies and talked about the school they were going to start. Sometimes they argued. I could tell they were very excited. While the people carried on, we three dogs lay with our muzzles on our paws and tried to stay cool.

"I'm not sure how healthy this climate is going to be for German shepherds," Jack said, giving the three of us a look of concern.

"They'll be fine," Morris said. "I give Buddy lots of water to drink and make sure she takes naps in the heat of the day."

Things were very busy after our friends arrived in town. Morris got his own office with a desk and a machine called a typewriter, which he used to tap out messages. Jack and a friend from "up North" named Willi found a building to use for kennels and training. Willi helped Jack find good dogs, and Jack and Adelaide started working with them. Morris spent a lot of time in his office, but every few days, he and I would walk over to the school to watch the training. Slowly, the dogs were learning.

Morris said to me, "School is finally in session, Buddy—and we couldn't have done it without you. You showed everyone what a smart dog can do."

Two blind men from Georgia and Illinois were in the first class of the school—which they now officially called The Seeing Eye. The men were paired with Gala and Tartar. Soon, all four of them were out on the streets, and suddenly, Morris and I weren't the only Seeing Eye Team in the world.

More people came to train every year. By the sixth year, fifty-seven people and their dogs were enrolled. Jack and Adelaide and Willi and Morris had their hands full.

I was lying on the floor next to Morris's desk one day when Jack banged into the office holding up a piece of paper.

"Guess what I've got here, Morris?" Jack said. "It's an invitation for you and Buddy to go to the White House and meet the president of the United States."

Morris jumped up and said, "No kidding! That's swell news. Did you hear that, Buddy? The president wants to meet you."

I had no idea what Morris was talking about, but I had a feeling it meant we were going to be taking another train ride.

Sure enough, some time later, Morris woke up one morning and shined his shoes and put on a tie and jacket. He whistled while we walked to the railroad station.

"We're going to Washington, to meet President Hoover, Buddy!" Morris said.

Morris told everyone on the train where we were going. Those people got just as excited as Morris. Some of them patted me and said, "Congratulations, Buddy." Or, "Say hi to Herbert Hoover for me."

When we got off the train, we rode in a horseless carriage. Morris proudly told the driver to take us to 1600 Pennsylvania Avenue.

"We're going to meet President Hoover," he told the driver.

The president's house was bigger than the Lady Boss's, with a wide green lawn stretching out in front of it. Lots of people in the big white house made a fuss over Morris and me. The president

shook Morris's hand and then patted me on the
head. Light boxes flashed lightning in my face.
I turned my head away so I wouldn't get those
spots in my vision. But the president looked right

into the lights. He didn't seem to mind. Maybe he was used to it.

"We are entering a new era for the blind," said President Hoover.

Beside me, I felt Morris swell up with pride. I gazed past the president and out the window at the green lawn and wondered what it would feel like to shake off my Working Harness and roll in the grass.

Happy Birthday, Buddy

Eventually, we moved The Seeing Eye up North to a place called New Jersey, where the summers were cooler and easier on us dogs. Morris and I went on many other trips to cities where he and I showed people how we worked together. Morris told me that when people met me and saw me in action, they wanted to give money to The Seeing Eye school. More money to the school meant more dogs to guide more blind people. But no matter how many dogs we trained, more were needed. Guide dogs for the blind were in high demand. The guide dogs who followed Gala and Tartar and me weren't just German shepherds. Some of them were golden retrievers and Labrador retrievers.

I was always happy to take Morris on fund-raising trips, but I will admit that there were days when I would have preferred to stay home and take it easy.

One day, Morris was getting ready to go out. He took my Working Harness off the hook. I got up slowly. I was getting along in years and not as spry as I used to be. I shook myself out and walked over so Morris could get me ready.

"What's wrong, girl?" Morris said. "Not feeling up to it today?"

At first, I was insulted. I was a working dog.

I was *always* ready to work. But lately, I did sometimes just want to lie down and rest.

Another day, Morris put on my Working Harness and walked me into the living room of our home. The room was filled with all my friends from the school, dogs and people. There were reporters there, too, with those flashing light boxes of theirs that, by now, I was pretty used to.

"Surprise!" everyone called out. "Happy birthday!"

But Morris didn't look the least bit surprised. He looked down at me. "It's not my birthday, Buddy. This is *your* day."

Now I was the one who looked surprised. *Who, me?*

I felt almost bashful. Everyone's eyes were on me as they sang. "Happy birthday, dear Buddy. Happy birthday to you!"

They clapped and cheered. On a low table, there was a lump of meat with a biscuit on top.

"Look, Buddy!" said Morris. "We made this birthday cake just for you, girl. It's one hundred percent chopped sirloin, with a dog-biscuit crust, and it's all for you. Dig in, girl!"

I looked up at Morris. He was pointing toward the meat. Everybody was looking at me. Everybody seemed to want me to eat it.

Really? I wondered. *For me?*

"No dog ever deserved it more," Morris said.

The reporters got down on their knees and snapped my picture. "Give us a smile, Buddy!" one of them said.

"Ladies and gentlemen," Morris said, "you see before you a very special lady. This is Buddy. She's *my* buddy, my guide, my partner, and the greatest dog in the whole wide world."

In case you are wondering, I, Buddy—the greatest dog in the whole wide world—ate the meat cake, biscuit and all. And after that, my belly full, I lay on a rug before the fire and chewed on a rubber ball.

"You've earned the rest, Buddy," said Morris.

I stopped chewing long enough to think about all the years Morris and I had worked together as a Team. Maybe he was right. Maybe I did deserve a rest . . . but only until tomorrow, when I knew I would strap on my Working Harness once more, and go on guiding Morris Frank wherever he wanted to go.

APPENDIX

More About the German Shepherd

German Shepherds in History

German shepherds are large dogs that come in a variety of colors, though most are tan and black. They are strong, alert, intelligent, and confident dogs with domed foreheads and square black muzzles.

The German shepherd breed dates back to the late 1880s, when a former German Army cavalry officer named Max von Stephanitz thought that a dog then known as an Alsatian sheepdog, which was bred to herd sheep, could learn to do other jobs. Von Stephanitz admired one such dog at a show. He bought it and renamed it Horand von Grafrath. He later founded the German Shepherd Dog Club, with Horand being the founding canine member. Von Stephanitz believed that it was more important for a dog to be useful than to look a certain way, so he devised certain tests that dogs had to pass in order to breed with the other dogs in the club. The tests involved obedience, tracking, and protection. Horand was bred to other, similarly talented dogs, which eventually led to the all-purpose working dog we know today. It's interesting to note that the club breeding logs also recorded four crosses with wolves!

Later, during World War I, the German Army used German shepherds as messenger dogs and rescue dogs. After the war, the army introduced shepherds as guides to veterans who had lost their sight in battle. These were the first guide dogs in modern times.

For more information about the breed, visit the German Shepherd Dog Club of America at gsdca.org.

The History of Guide Dogs

It was the work of these German Army dogs that gave Mrs. Dorothy Eustis the idea to train dogs exclusively to guide the blind. On her estate in Switzerland, she worked with Jack Humphrey, a geneticist and dog trainer, to teach German shepherds the skills they needed to lead the blind. Morris Frank was the first student to take one of her dogs. The dog was originally named Kiss, but Morris renamed her Buddy. With Mrs. Eustis's money and support, Morris Frank was able to open the first school for The Seeing Eye in Nashville on January 29, 1929. When Buddy died, shortly after her tenth birthday, Morris named his next dog Buddy II.

For more information about The Seeing Eye, visit seeingeye.org.

For more information about Morris Frank and Buddy, including photographs and a video, visit aph.org/hall_fame/bios/frank.html.

Morris Frank returning to Nashville from Vevey, Switzerland, with Buddy on June 12, 1928

Jack Humphrey training Gala

Dorothy Harrison Eustis

Morris Frank training with Buddy in Switzerland

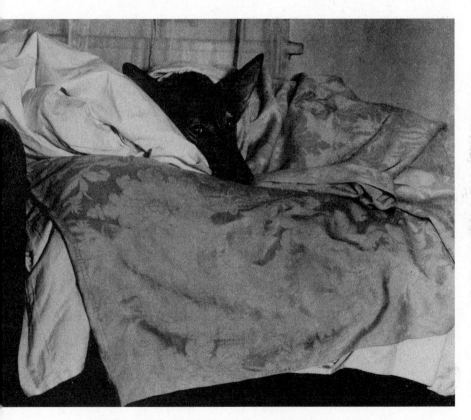

Buddy recuperating from an illness in December 1937

Training Guide Dogs

Today there are guide dog schools all over the country, but they operate much the same way as The Seeing Eye. Most schools breed their own dogs: German shepherds, Labrador retrievers, boxers, golden retrievers, and Lab-golden crosses are the most common breeds.

When a dog is eight weeks old, it is placed in the home of a volunteer puppy raiser, where it is exposed to affection, obedience training, and a variety of social situations.

When the dog is between fourteen and eighteen months old, it returns to the school and begins a training course with a sighted instructor that lasts four to six months.

During training, the dog learns such basic commands as Forward, Right, and Left, as well as Intelligent Disobedience.

When a dog graduates from this stage, it is matched with a blind person. For about a month, an instructor works with the human-dog team before the dog goes home to live with its new master. Guide dogs work, on average, for six to eight years and then retire, often to adoptive homes where they are allowed to relax for the rest of their lives. Guiding is intense work, and these dogs have earned their rest.

Hosting Guide Puppies

In order to become a puppy raiser for The Seeing Eye, you must join a 4-H/Seeing Eye puppy-raising club and attend regular meetings. Being a puppy raiser involves taking a puppy into your home, loving it, caring for it, giving it some basic obedience training, and taking it out in public so it gets used to all sorts of people and social situations. Most importantly, guide puppy hosts must be emotionally prepared to return the dogs to the school once the training period is over.

For a list of guide dog schools organized by state, visit the National Federation of the Blind at nfb.org/resource-list-guide-dog-schools.

Read on for the beginning of the next

DOG DIARIES

BOOK

I'm Barry. People say I saved over forty lives.

Many call me a hero, but I just think of myself as a dog who loved the snow—to walk in it, to roll in it, and to search for people buried under it.

BARRY

Based on a true story!

1

LITTLE BEAR

My name is Barry der Menschenretter. That's MEN-shun-RET-uh. A big name, you say? Well, in life, I was a big dog. If you want to see me with your own eyes, go to the Natural History Museum in Bern, Switzerland. There you will see my stuffed body in a glass case. I apologize in advance for my appearance. They repaired me and patched me and added fur and stuffing in 1923, raising my head to show me in a less humble pose. In spite of all their efforts, I no longer look very much like myself. But perhaps you can see something of the original dog in me if you look carefully and imagine.

I come from a long line of big dogs called mastiffs. Mastiffs marched and fought with the Roman army in ancient times. Even before that, there were mastiffs in a faraway place called Tibet, where they were said to guard sacred temples. In modern times, my kind of mastiff is called a Saint Bernard, but in the year 1800, when my story begins, there were no such things as Saint Bernards. Dogs such as I were called *Alpenhunde,* a German word that means "dogs from the Alps"— the high mountain range in Switzerland, a country in western Europe. People also called us butcher's dogs, perhaps because we need to eat over two pounds of meat a day and only a butcher could afford to keep us.

But the most common name for us dogs was bari. *Bari* means "little bear" in Swiss German. That's what my name means: Little Bear. With my thick fur and big, padded feet—like a bear—I was well suited to living in the cold.

The place in the Alps where I lived is so high there is snow on the ground sometimes year-round. It is 8,000 feet above sea level. Today, people have learned to master the snow. They plow through it in vehicles with special wheels and shovels. They fly over it in silver birds called airplanes. They even play in it, sliding down it on sleds and on skinny sticks called skis. But in my day, before special vehicles or skis, snow was a very serious matter. In fact, where I came from, people called snow the White Death.

Today, there is a tunnel bored through solid rock that is a shortcut from one side of the Alps to the other. But in my day, there was no tunnel. People who needed to get from Switzerland to Italy had to climb over the Alps on foot or ride on mules. When the steep mountains got buried in snow, the going became difficult—and sometimes impossible. Almost as bad as the snow were the swirling banks of fog. People froze. They got lost. They got buried alive in avalanches.

What is an avalanche? An avalanche is a great big spill of snow, rocks, and ice that comes thundering down a mountainside as if some giant has sent it tumbling. Avalanches are unpredictable things and have many causes. Sometimes when the temperature rises there is a sudden thaw, causing wet, heavy snow to slide. Other times, a new layer of fresh snow slips down the face of an older layer of snow. However it comes about, if you happen to be standing in the way of an avalanche, you are out of luck. There is no time to escape.

That is where we baris came in. Our job was to guide the lost, to warm up the frozen, and to find those buried alive. In my lifetime, they say I rescued over forty travelers from the White Death. They say I was a hero. But I say I simply loved the snow. I loved to walk in it. I loved to roll in it. I loved to search for people buried under it. If it is heroic to do what you love—and to do it well—then I guess I was a hero. But I prefer to think of myself as a Dog at Home in the Snow.